THUMPY FEET

THUMPY FEET

by Betsy Lewin

Holiday House / New York

Library of Congress Cataloging-in-Publication Data
Lewin, Betsy, author, illustrator.
Thumpy Feet / by Betsy Lewin. — First edition.
pages cm
Summary: "Thumpy thumpy thumpy thump thumpy.
Spend a day with Thumpy Feet, a spirited orange cat"— Provided by publisher.
ISBN 978-0-8234-2901-1 (hardcover)
1. Cats—Juvenile fiction. [1. Cats—Fiction.] I. Title.
PZ10.3.L564Th 2013
[E]—dc23
2012045826

ISBN 978-0-8234-3174-8 (paperback)

For Gaby

Here comes Thumpy Feet!

Thumpy

thumpy

thumpy

thump

thumpy

MMMMMMMmmmmmmm

Foodie food!

Smacky smacky

smack

smacky

smack

Licky lick!

Licky licky

lick

lick licky licky

LOOKY LOOK!

Mousy mouse!

POUNCY POUNCE!

Flippy FLIP

flip

flippy

flippy

flip

flip

YAA

Noddy

nod

Noddy

noddy

noddy

nod

SNOOZY SNOOZE

Snoozy snoozy snoooozy

LOOKY LOOK!

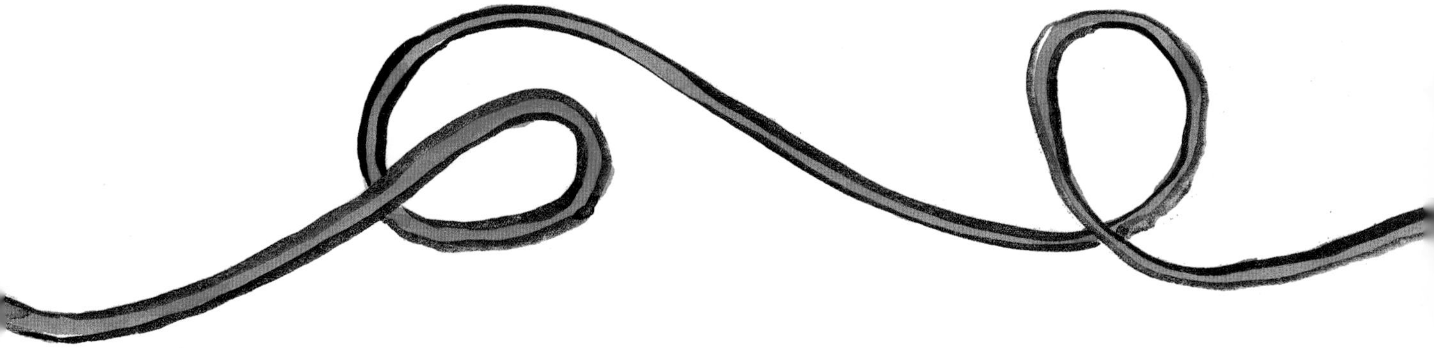

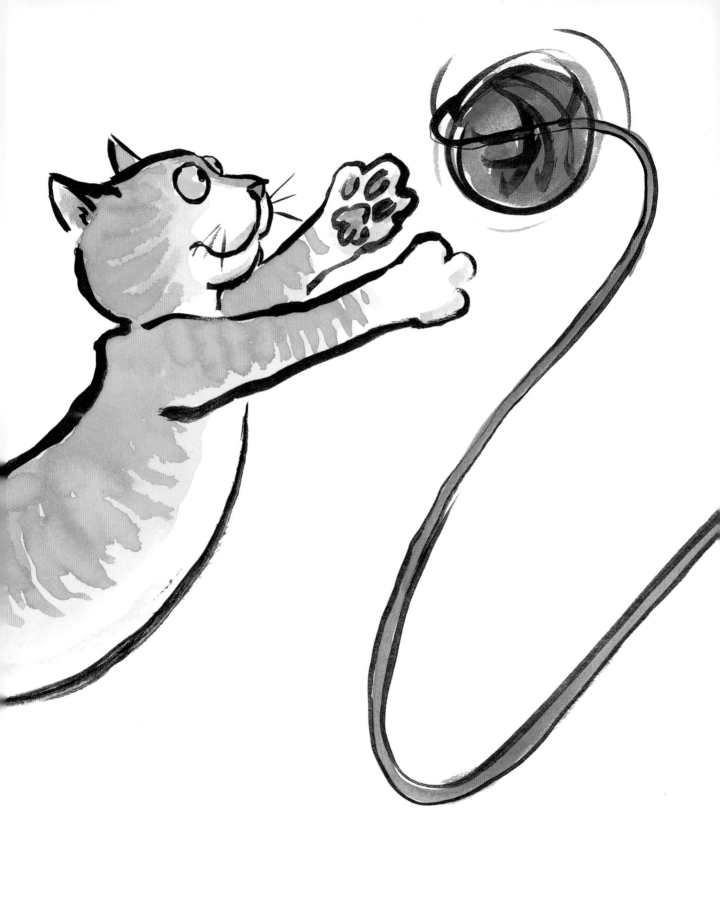